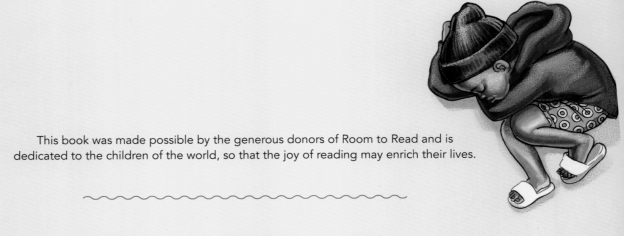

This book was made possible by the generous donors of Room to Read and is dedicated to the children of the world, so that the joy of reading may enrich their lives.

Written by Godfrey Mishomari and Amon Majaliwa
Illustrated by Cloud Chatanda
Edited by Alfredo Santos
Designed by Riaan Muller Coetzee
Design Adaptation by Janet Pagliuca
Art Director: Riaan Muller Coetzee
Editorial Director: Carol Burrell

First published in 2023 by Room to Read in Tanzania

ISBN 979-8-4000-0275-5
Manufactured in Canada

Room to Read
465 California Street #1000
San Francisco, California 94104
www.roomtoread.org

**Room
to
Read**

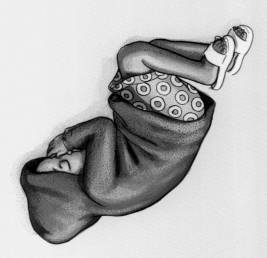

KADOGOO is EveryWHERE

by

Godfrey Mishomari and
Amon Majaliwa

illustrated by

Cloud Chatanda

Kadogoo lived in a big home with many other children. Every week on visiting day, people came to meet them.

Sometimes, one of the children went to live with a new family.

4

Another visiting day came and went.
No one asked to meet Kadogoo.

"One day people will know my name,"
he said. "Everyone will know Kadogoo."

"If you want to be remembered, Kadogoo," said Lisa, "do something everybody will remember."

6

Kadogoo went to the library.
"Everyone will remember me here," he said.

on the doors . . .

and on the floors.

Kadogoo went outside.

He scratched his name into the tree . . .

onto a rock . . .

and even on an old car in the grass.

One day, someone erased all his names.

"Who did this? I will catch them. I will set a trap!"

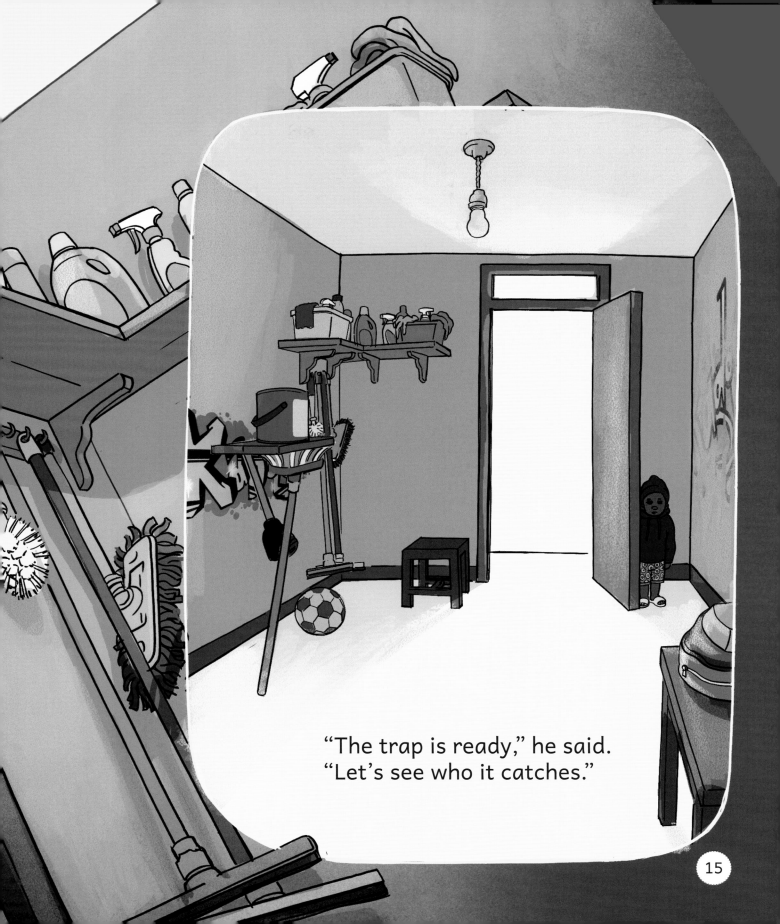

"The trap is ready," he said.
"Let's see who it catches."

Kadogoo waited . . .

and waited . . .

and waited some more.

He was so tired of waiting.

"Oops! Aaaaah! Oh nooo!"

"Oh no, it's Kadogoo," said Lisa.

"Oh yes, it's Kadogoo!" said the other children. They laughed and laughed.

"We don't want your name everywhere!"

"I'm sorry," said Kadogoo.
"I just want everyone
to remember me."

"Come on, Kadogoo," said Lisa. "I'll help you clean."

He remembered
a book he read.

LIBRARY

"I'll try something new."

THE POWER OF ART

He made the walls beautiful.

One day, a family saw Kadogoo's paintings.
"Can we meet Kadogoo?" they asked.

They enjoyed the visit so much!
"We will visit you again, Kadogoo,"
they told him.

Now everyone knew him.

And no one ever forgot Kadogoo.

Godfrey Mishomari

Godfrey Mishomari is an author and an editor, and likes both reading and writing. *Kadogoo Is Everywhere* is one of his favorite works. His other books are *Lisa anapenda Kucheza*, *Siku yangu ya Kuzaliwa*, *Kadogoo afanya mabadiliko*, *Maputo*, and *Mbuni*.

Amon Majaliwa

Amon Majaliwa is a communicator in creative writing and visual arts based in Dar es Salaam. He works in sculpture, drawings, paintings, and creative writing, just to name a few. Amon participated in Room to Read's Global Writers and Illustrators Workshop, and *Kadogoo Is Everywhere* is his first collaborative book.

Cloud Chatanda

Cloud Chatanda is a freelance illustrator whose passion for drawing started when he was young. Cloud received art training from Kinondoni Young Artist (KYA). He has worked with various publishers on many books in Tanzania. His first illustrated books were *Bahati na Mumewe*, *Vitendawili kwa picha*, and *Binti Chura na Mwanasimba Hali Mbala*. Cloud has participated in several Room to Read Workshops, where he previously illustrated *Thandi and Muno* and *Cut Tree—Plant Tree*.

Room to Read

Room to Read seeks to transform the lives of millions of children through education, to create a world free from illiteracy and gender inequality. We envision a world where all children have room to read, learn, and grow and can use their skills to accelerate positive change.

Founded in 2000 on the belief that World Change Starts with Educated Children®, Room to Read has published more than 4,400 children's and young adult book titles through its programs and has distributed more than 39 million books in 23 countries, providing students and educators in over 192,000 communities with resources and guidance to build a strong foundation in literacy and a love of reading.

Learn more at www.roomtoread.org

CHILDREN in CARE

COLLECTION

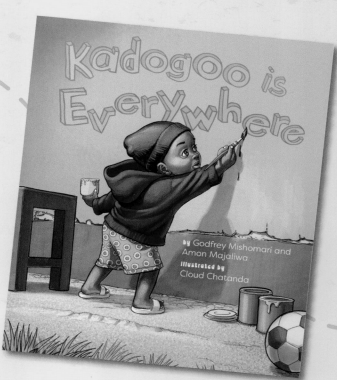

Kadogoo is Everywhere

by Godfrey Mishomari and
Amon Majaliwa

Illustrated by
Cloud Chatanda

Room to Read's **fourth global children's book collection** brings children who live in different types of foster care around the world to the forefront of their own stories. Our goal is to provide an opportunity for all children to read stories that reflect these diverse experiences and that present futures of possibilities, and to create bonding between children and their supportive adults as they engage with the stories together. The stories we share can help all of us learn to navigate relationships, build trust and a sense of security, and reimagine family.

For the global collection, authors and illustrators created books for Cambodia, Vietnam, Laos, Nepal, India, Bangladesh, Tanzania, South Africa, Sri Lanka, and the United States. The collection celebrates the many ways we grow a home.